ISBN: 978-1-7348258-5-5 (paperback)
978-1-7348258-6-2 (hardback)
978-1-7348258-4-8 (ebook)

Library of Congress Control Number:

Illustrations by Pardeep Mehra
Book Design by Praise Saflor

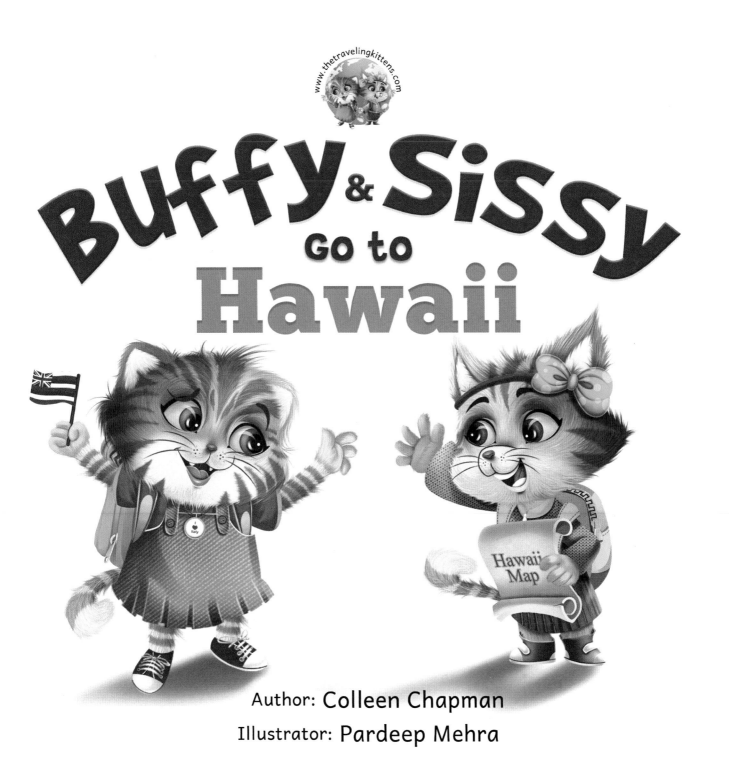

Buffy & Sissy Go to Hawaii

Author: Colleen Chapman

Illustrator: Pardeep Mehra

This book belongs to:

"It's vacation time!" Buffy and Sissy are excited.
Mama tells the kittens to pack their toothbrushes, bathing suits and suntan lotion.
"I can't forget my camera," adds Sissy.

The kittens stuff their backpacks.
Sissy grabs her camera.
They are ready for the
long flight to Hawaii.

Mama reads from her travel guide,
"The state of Hawaii is made up of eight islands.
We are going to three—Oahu, The Big Island of Hawaii and Maui."
Sissy is excited and says, "I'll be able to take a lot of
photos," as she snaps a picture of the clouds.

After a long plane ride, they arrive on the island of Oahu and a lady places flowers around their necks.

"Why did we get flowers?" asks Buffy. "These are called *leis*," answers Mama. "In Hawaii, visitors are often given *leis* as a welcome greeting."

The kittens inhale the sweet smell of the tropical flowers.

As they settle into the hotel room, the kittens chat about what they will do in Hawaii. "I want to take pictures of sea animals and make a collage for my bedroom," says Sissy. Buffy's list includes seeing a volcano and trying shave ice. Sissy laughs, "Your list *would* include something to eat!"

"Would you like to try surfing, girls?" Mama asks.
"I want to learn, but it looks so hard!" Sissy answers.
"It looks easy to me," says Buffy, "but where's the shave ice?"

At the beach, Buffy & Sissy meet their surfing instructor, Koa. He greets the kittens warmly. "Aloha and welcome to Hawaii!" After their lesson, the kittens run into the ocean with their surfboards.

"Look, Sissy! I'm surfing!" squeals Buffy as she gets up on the board her very first try while Sissy loses her balance and splashes into the water. "This is too hard," Sissy says, starting to cry. But with a little encouragement from Koa, she tries again.

Bravely, and a bit wobbly, Sissy gets back on her board. As a big wave comes behind her, she quickly paddles to catch it. She stands up and rides to shore with a big smile on her face.

After the surfing lesson, Koa teaches them Hawaiian words like *aloha* and *mahalo*. He also shows them how to do the *shaka* hand sign.

"I'm getting so hot. Can we get some shave ice?" asks Buffy. "Follow me," replies Koa.

The shave ice stand has so many delicious flavors. Sissy picks strawberry and Buffy chooses pineapple. Koa decides on blue coconut and Mama gets her favorite—cherry.

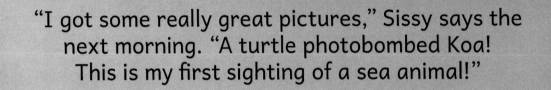

"I got some really great pictures," Sissy says the
next morning. "A turtle photobombed Koa!
This is my first sighting of a sea animal!"

18

Buffy laughs and says, "I'm getting hungry.
Can we have shave ice for breakfast?"
Mama says, "Let's have a healthy breakfast first."
The kittens eat their oatmeal and pineapple
and get ready for their next adventure.

Mama and the kittens fly to another island
called The Big Island of Hawaii.
The kittens are thrilled to see the Kilauea
volcano at the Hawaii Volcanoes National Park.

"This is awesome," says Buffy. "It looks like we are on the moon." The park ranger tells the kittens that astronauts actually trained at the park. Buffy imagines herself as an astronaut floating above the park.

That evening Mama has a surprise. They are going to a luau. Mama explains that a luau is a big feast with lots of food, Hawaiian music and dancing. After dinner, the kittens get a hula lesson.

There's much more to see on The Big Island. Mama and the kittens take a boat tour along the Kona coastline to look for dolphins. The kittens put on snorkel gear and Sissy grabs her underwater camera.

As soon as they see dolphins, the kittens jump into the water. One of the dolphins stops and looks right at Sissy. She quickly snaps a picture.

When they are back aboard the boat Sissy says, "I think the dolphin wants to be my friend! She was smiling at me!"

Buffy laughs. "Dolphins always look like they're smiling!"

Later that night, they visit Keauhou Bay to see large sea animals called manta rays who are often found in warm tropical waters. They notice people holding onto surfboards and shining lights into the water. Mama explains. "The lights attract *plankton* that the manta rays like to eat. They are gentle and curious and won't hurt you, but don't touch them."

Buffy and Sissy put on snorkel gear and hold on tight to surfboards as they search under the water. A large manta ray swims toward them with its mouth wide open and scoops up the plankton.

Buffy hollers, "I can't believe how close it was to us! I didn't touch it but it almost touched me."

The adventure continues on the island of Maui as Mama and the kittens go on a whale watching tour. The boat captain explains that the humpback whales migrate from cold Alaska to warm Hawaii in the winter months to have their babies. Sissy spots a whale jumping out of the water.
"Look Mama! She has a baby with her."

All too soon, it is time to fly home. Mama surprises the kittens with special charms to add to their backpacks— a dolphin for Sissy and a manta ray for Buffy.

Back on the airplane, Sissy says, "Look at my pictures of all the sea animals! I have a whale, a dolphin, a manta ray and a sneaky turtle!"

Buffy is fast asleep, happily dreaming of shave ice and surfboards. The kittens can't wait for their next adventure!

Did you know that the characters of Buffy & Sissy are based on real cats? Buffy and Sissy are tabby sisters who live with their human mama!

Meet Buffy

Meet Sissy

Photos by Antonio Crutchley

HAWAII

Kauai
Oahu
Molokai
Lanai
Maui
Hawaii

Words that Buffy & Sissy learned in Hawaii

Lei	~ Flowers	**Buffy**	~ Hawaiian name Pupi
Aloha	~ Hello and Goodbye	**Sissy**	~ Hawaiian name Kiki
Mahalo	~ Thank you	**Home**	~ Hale
Luau	~ A Hawaiian feast	**Mother**	~ Makuahine
Hula	~ Hawaiian dance	**Father**	~ Makua kane
Shaka sign	~ Symbol of Aloha (hang loose)	**Family**	~ Ohana

Please visit **www.thetravelingkittens.com** to download your **free activity and coloring sheets** of
Buffy and Sissy's trip to Hawaii!

Follow Buffy & Sissy on social media!

thetravelingkittens2

The Traveling Kittens

Giving back is important to
Buffy & Sissy. A portion of the profits of
this series will go towards
charities to help animals.

Share this book with your friends!

Made in the USA
Las Vegas, NV
30 July 2021